For Willow, Eliza, Monty, Oliver, Angus, Ben, Albie, and Kitty. Let's party!—A.C.

For my sister—R.A.

The
Cow That Was the Best
M o o - t h e r
Text copyright © 2009 by Andy Cutbill
Illustrations copyright © 2009 by Russell Ayto
Manufactured in China. All rights reserved.
No part of this book may be used or reproduced in any
manner whatsoever without written permission except in
the case of brief quotations embodied in critical articles and
reviews. For information address HarperCollins Children's Books,
a division of HarperCollins Publishers, 1350 Avenue
of the Americas, New York, NY 10019.
www.harpercollinschildrens.com
Library of Congress Cataloging-in-Publication Data is available.
ISBN 978-0-06-166472-4 (trade bdg.)
1   2   3   4   5   6   7   8   9   10
❖ First American Edition, 2009
Originally published in Great Britain
by HarperCollins Children's Books,
2 0 0 9

The COW That was the BEST Moo-ther

by Andy Cutbill

illustrated by Russell Ayto

HarperCollinsPublishers

One morning
Marjorie the cow
woke with a jolt.

The farmer's wife was hammering
up a poster in the yard.

BANG! BANG!

BEAUTIFUL
BABY
CONTEST

THIS AFTERNOON

STRICTLY

"It's a beautiful baby contest!"
read Derek the bull.
"This afternoon. STRICTLY cows only."
"OOOOOOOOh,"
said the lady cows.
They were extremely excited.
So was Marjorie. . . .

Her baby, Daisy, had
been a special cow since the very
moment she'd hatched
from an *egg*!

Mom and Baby

OOS OF THE WORLD

Eggstraordinary

COW LAYS EGG

Farme

chicken ns cow eggs chicl
ns cow eggs chicl
y eggs chicl
chicl

"All my own work," said Farmer.

HOLY COW!

Daisy sleeping yesterday

First Hoofprint

" said a chicken.

All the baby cows started
practicing for the contest.

Their moms taught them
to **SWISH** their tails . . .

trot up   and down . . .

and mooooo delightfully.

Marjorie wanted to help Daisy.

But Daisy was too busy
with the chickens.

Soon it was time
for the contest to begin.
Derek herded the
spectators into the yard.
"Good luck, Marge!"
called the chickens.

everywhere!

A nervous hush fell over the barn as the farmer's wife appeared.

Carefully she studied the babies,

checking behind their ears and trotting them around the yard a bit.

Finally she reached Daisy.
Marjorie felt very proud.
But as the farmer's wife
bent down, Daisy noticed
something wriggling
in her hat. . . .

A big, fat, juicy worm.

The farmer's wife turned green.

"A ch-ch-chicken!"

she spluttered.

And she
fainted.

THUMP!

Marjorie scooped Daisy into her arms.
"Daisy might not be like your babies," she said,
"but she's mine, and I love her!"

Well, you could almost hear a pin drop.

"Glad to hear it,"
said Derek all of a sudden.

And he promptly
slapped a large award
on Marjorie's chest.

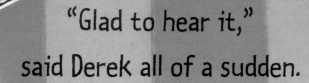

"Best in Show,"
he said.
"For being the world's
best mom!"

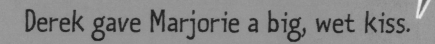

Derek gave Marjorie a big, wet kiss.

"Ahhhh," sighed the chickens.
And Marjorie blushed all over.